# SEAL'S DESPERATE LITTLE

## Age Play DDlg Romance

### Amanda King

ISBN: 9798846159792
Imprint: Independently published

1st edition

Cover design by: Amanda King

# CONTENTS

# CHAPTER 1

*Gloria*

The sun, so hot and so bright in the sky, shining light on my face. I hid it with my arm, making my way to my car. It was parked in front of the café where I worked. Around me, not many people perambulating on the streets. Only a couple of stragglers here and there.

I reached my car and opened the door. After sitting down, I already felt a lot more comfortable and better about everything. Even though I kind of liked working in that café, it wasn't for me and I didn't think it would ever be. I wished to be doing something different with my life.

Something more grandiose, maybe traveling around the world, meeting new people, new cultures, and doing all that with someone important to me. Someone that I could call my love.

I shook my head, closing my eyes tightly.

I doubted that any of those things would happen. I was stuck here in Sudbury. The town was nice, but it was too small. More and more, that was what I always thought, and I couldn't change it.

One of the reasons why I thought my life would always remain this way was because I was a Little. Always had been. Ever since I was just a teen, when I was still a child, I always saw myself with different eyes. I had always liked to play with my toys, always liked to watch cartoons, and be someone else from who society wanted me to be.

I took a deep breath and reopened my eyes. At least, here I had a house. It wasn't big and it certainly would never impress anyone, but it was my place. The good thing about living in Sudbury was that saving up money was easy, even though I didn't make much.

My expenses here were minimal. The house itself had been a gift from my late parents. They passed away a long time ago. I was still a young teen when it happened. When they died, my aunt took care of me, and she was the most important person in the world to me.

She was so important that I always told her everything about my life, including the fact that the house now had a playroom with a huge crib in it. Most people, upon finding out about that, would have stopped talking to me and maybe even called the police on me, but not her. She was different. She was more willing to accept things that challenged her understanding of the world.

I turned the key in the ignition, thinking that the engine of the car was going to turn on, but it didn't. It made a sound that suggested it was dead, but it didn't make me feel scared that the engine wasn't going to work. In fact, this was far from the first time something like this was happening. There had been so many times when the engine died on me, and I knew I just needed to turn the key one more time so that it finally worked.

And that I did, hoping that it was going to achieve the result I wanted, but then I was disappointed when it didn't. I squinted my eyes slowly, looking at the console and finding out that nothing appeared to be wrong with any part of the car, including the engine. If something was wrong with it, it would be showing me so right now.

"What the hell's going on with you?" I asked, shaking my head in disbelief. I couldn't believe that I was going to have to step out of the car and pop open the engine compartment.

No pointing in delaying it, I thought after opening the door and then going to the front of the car. Just when I was going to pop open the lid, I noticed footsteps approaching me.

Then, I turned around and found someone that made my body feel hot all over, and I didn't know why. Or maybe I did and I didn't want to admit it to myself.

The man was hot. He was stunning, jaw-dropping, and that was putting it mildly. I just didn't think that someone like him was living here in Sudbury. Where had he been all this time? I asked myself, realizing that I was pushing my body against the frame of the car.

Why was I feeling so submissive and small in his presence?

Again, the reason for that was typical. Just like so many other men I had seen in my life, both here in Sudbury and on TV, I was beginning to develop a crush on him.

Of course that was what I was going to be feeling. It wasn't just the fact that he was stunning and so tall, but also that his body was… Well, suffice to say that it made me want to see him naked. I couldn't help but wonder what he was like without his clothes on.

But I knew that would never happen, so I was smashing my hopes right at this moment. No point in building false hope, especially when there was a good chance that he wasn't even coming in my direction. Maybe he was just going to walk past me, and if that happened, it wouldn't be a surprise.

After all, why would anyone – and especially someone of his caliber – even look twice at me?

But that was the thing. Whoever he was, he was staring right at me, and that was only making my body feel hotter. I felt like I was running a fever, and I was certain that he was thinking I looked funny. If that was the case, I wouldn't blame him.

I just hoped that I was going to stop whatever was happening here before I made a fool of myself.

He stopped when he was no more than a couple of feet from me. I could see it in his face and eyes. He wasn't someone that had never left Sudbury. He had gone elsewhere, perhaps even out of the country. He had this vibe around him that he had seen things he didn't want to share with anyone. Some scars painted his face, and even though he was Caucasian like I was, his skin had faint but visible signs that he had been under the sun for years in a faraway country.

"Do you need help with anything?"

And his voice was like music to my ears.

# CHAPTER 2

*Sydney*

When I spotted her from afar, I knew she was having problems with her car. Or maybe that she was going to have a problem with it in the next couple of seconds. I had spotted her even before she stepped out of the car. I had spotted her through the windshield. Something was different about her. Something that I couldn't put my finger on, especially for someone like me that wasn't looking for a relationship.

So, why the hell did I grow so interested in her all of a sudden? I didn't know, but there was no point in stopping what was already happening anyway, so I couldn't just walk away.

"Yeah, I think I do. I think that my car just broke down," she replied, and then she added, "my name is Gloria. I've never seen you around here before. Are you new in town?"

I was indeed new here in town, and it was a surprise to me that she noticed it so soon. Was it really so obvious? I asked myself, my eyes going up and down, scrutinizing every part of her body, though without making it so obvious. I didn't want her to think I was some kind of rapist or anything of the sort.

It was just that she was jaw-dropping and made my cock hard under my pants. Still, I was of course controlling it so that it wasn't too obvious. If she looked down, she would certainly notice my growing bulge. Not much I could do about that other than turning around and leaving, but I wasn't going to do that, of course.

"I am, yeah. My name is Sydney," I said, shaking her hand slightly. I wished we could do more than that, but I wasn't going to complain. The fact that I felt her skin touching mine, her fingers interlaced with mine, was already good enough. I missed it already that they weren't connected anymore, though.

Gloria chuckled, pushing her hair behind her ear. She was nervous. She was snow-white and her cheeks blushed easily even though not much was happening right now. How much she wanted me was more than obvious, though, of course, I wasn't going to bring it up – not right now, anyway.

I had come here with a mission in mind and I was going to fulfill my duty as someone that should help her. After all, she looked like someone who needed a helping hand right now.

"Well, Sydney, it's pretty nice to meet you," she turned around, showing me the back of her body, and it was even more mouthwatering than the front. I had to stop myself from lunging at her and running my hands all over her curves. I could just imagine her being a Little, someone that I could settle on my lap and murmur into her ear that she was the most special person in the world to me. "And as you can see, I think that my car really has broken down. I don't understand anything about engines, so if you could help me with it, I would be relieved."

"Let me see what's wrong with it," I said, putting my hands under the lid and popping it open, my eyes scanning the engine. It wasn't going to take much time. Something that I mastered while I was a SEAL was fixing engines. It wasn't a part of my main assignments, but it was always present in my duties.

Some minutes later, I said, "Aha, this is easy. You just need to do this," I said, making sure that I was doing this slowly. I wanted her to learn from me. So, I moved some parts of the engine here and there, making sure that everything was in the right places, and then I closed the engine compartment, dusting off my hands.

"There. Try it again. I think that the engine is going to work now."

"Really? It was so simple?" She asked, smiling from ear to ear. She went around the vehicle, sat in the driver's seat, and then turned the key again, and, this time, it worked. The engine started to rumble and whir. I felt good about this.

"Thank you so much," she said and I went around the vehicle.

"It was nothing. I was a SEAL until not too long ago and before that, I was a mechanic. I know how to fix engines, so it wasn't hard for me to figure out what was wrong with your car."

My hand went into the pocket of my pants and I got a small piece of paper from my notebook. I liked to take it around with me in case I needed to give my number to someone. I knew that she could just type it down on her phone, but that didn't have the same charm as what I was doing right now.

"Here," I said, giving her the small piece of paper. "If you need to call me for anything engine related, you have my number. I don't have a job right now, so you can call me pretty much anytime and I know that I would have enough time to help you."

She blinked twice, eventually getting the small piece of paper from my hand. Her hand was shaking, which wasn't surprising. I knew who I was and I was also aware of the 'effect' I had on women.

She looked up, her glistening eyes finding mine. "I'm going to make sure to save this on my contact list. Still, hopefully my engine will never break down again."

"You know that's just not possible. Eventually, it will stop working for whatever reason and you are going to need me."

"As long as you are still living here."

I pulled myself away from her car, saying, "I'm probably going to remain here for the time being. Like I said, not much going on in my life right now, so… Yeah. I guess I'll see you around."

She waved her hand, saying, "thank you again, and hopefully we'll see each other again."

And even though we didn't have many reasons to ever talk again, I knew that we would. I felt that we would. I felt that something important and deep was connecting us, and I was excited about it.

So excited that I felt slightly saddened that she was already leaving.

# CHAPTER 3

*Gloria*

I jumped out of my sedan feeling happier than normal. I didn't know why that was. Perhaps it was because I had seen him. Perhaps it was because we had talked. Perhaps it was because of his voice, which was so mesmerizing and it made my mind obsessed with it.

*But you're never even going to see him again*, I tried to tell myself, but it wasn't like my mind could just understand that so easily.

At least, I was finally home. When I had left the café, it was already dusk, but now it was dark. It always took some time until I got home. Now that I was here, I found myself so much more comfortable and welcomed. I felt like I could be my true self again and that nobody could judge me.

Which was certainly the case. Now that I was home, I could go to my playroom after taking a hot shower. I couldn't wait until I was under the showerhead and the water was flowing down my body.

I took a deep breath in and I realized that I still remembered his voice even though we hadn't talked much. His name was Sydney and he was stunning. When we shook hands, I felt how strong it was, and even though it was the most obvious thing to do, I didn't want to do it. I didn't want to pull my hand back.

I shouldn't have done that, now that I was thinking about it. I should've made it so we were kissing each other soon after that, but of course, I was just daydreaming, and it was much better for me that I just entered my house and pretended that everything was back to normal.

So, I entered my house, put my shoulder bag on the couch, and then took off my clothes, entering the bathroom a moment later. I turned on the showerhead and I stepped under it, the water flowing down my body. It was warm. It was good, and so much so that the only thing I wanted to do right now was to close my eyes and tune out everything around me. I didn't want to be thinking about anything that wasn't Sydney.

I had such a huge crush on him and I could just imagine him becoming my Daddy, even though I was certain that would never happen. I was certain because there was no way he was a Daddy. The moment when he found out that I was a Little, he would kick me out of his life so hard that I wouldn't be able to understand what was going on before it was too late.

Just when I was going to apply shampoo to my hair, I heard a weird noise coming from inside my house. Huh? I asked myself, stepping out from under the showerhead. I turned it off and then started to dry myself with a towel, in a moment realizing that I was just wasting time and that, if there was really someone who had broken into my house, then I had to get my phone right away and call the police.

Or maybe I should call Sydney. He would come here and kick the shit out of whoever was trying to rob me.

Without giving it a second thought, I walked out of the bathroom with my towel wrapped around my body. Just as I was doing that, I dodged a shadow lunging at me. It was an arm. An arm speeding through the air, aiming for my head, and I had just about enough time to do that before it was too late.

I threw my body the other way, whirling around when I found a man no more than some feet away from me. He straightened up his back, turning his body around so that I could see his face, and the moment when I did that, I gasped.

I never thought he would come back.

I never thought that he would manage to find me here.

But now that I was thinking about it, I realized I made a huge mistake. I shouldn't be living alone. I shouldn't be living here where he could find me so easily and hurt me.

"Gloria, it's so good to see you again."

That voice. I recognized it easily. He was my ex. He was my Daddy when I still thought there was love in the world. When I had thought that I was in love with him, but that was such a long time ago that nothing about it mattered anymore.

"What are you doing here?" I growled, stepping away from him. My phone was on the couch. That was where I had left it and, to get it, all I needed to do was to speed over to it as fast as my legs could take me.

And yet, the only problem with that was that I was certain he was much faster than me. He was bigger than me, but his heavier weight wasn't an obstacle. His legs were much stronger than mine and I knew that, if I chose the wrong move now, he wouldn't hesitate before hurting me.

"I came here for you. I'm still not over you."

And that was when I knew I didn't have much time to make my choice.

# CHAPTER 4

*Gloria*

So, I had to make a choice I had no idea if it was going to pan out or not. Without even thinking one more time about it, I dashed over to my phone on the couch, and just when I was with my fingers grabbing it, something heavy but soft shoved me away from it and I fell on my ass on the floor.

I looked up and found Jason glaring down at me. It was like he wanted to kill me right at this moment, and he could actually do that without a problem. His hand was holding a military-grade knife.

Even though he had knocked me down on the floor, there was still something I could do. Something that would change this for the better for me.

I was fast enough that I could call one of the numbers on my contact list. They were good people. Most of them were, anyway. The moment when they realized there was a call from me that they missed, they would call back. And when they realized that I wasn't picking up the phone, they would come here to check up on me.

At least, that was what I was hoping for.

"You're going to regret this!" I barked and he burst out laughing, showing me that he wasn't afraid of my threats at all.

"I didn't come here to kill you if that's what you are worried about," Jason explained, but whatever he had to say to me wasn't going to change anything.

911. I could call the police – or to be more precise about it, the local sheriff's department – but that would still mean typing all three numbers on the screen and if I did that, I would not know if I would have enough time to get away from this before it was too late.

After all, Jason was pointing the knife at me and I knew that he was capable of hurting me with it. That was why I wasn't going to wait until he finally passed out. He was drunk. Just like all the other times when he was like that, he was so drunk that he would eventually pass out and I would be able to tell Victor about what happened here. And only then would I feel safe enough.

But it was just like I had said. I didn't have time to type all three numbers on the screen. So, without even glancing down at it, I pressed my finger on Sydney's number, and that was all the time I had. The moment when I did that, Jason kicked my hand with all the strength he had, my phone flying to the other side of the living room.

It hurt. A lot. It hurt my hand more than I thought it was going to, and I suddenly found myself hating him so much. Now, more than ever, I wanted to see him dead.

"You're going to pay for this. I had once thought that I really loved you," I barked and he cackled, showing me that no matter what I said, it wasn't going to change him. It wasn't going to change his mind.

"Nobody is going to do anything against me. You are too weak to do anything that can hurt me. All you can do is keep spitting out the same shit over and over and, to be honest, that's quite pathetic. Looking at you now… I can't help but wonder how I fell in love with someone like you. I must've been out of my mind," he said, reaching down with his hands and grabbing me, his fingers digging deep into the skin of my arms. He pulled me up, letting the towel fall down to the floor. It exposed my body to his eyes, which were quick to check me out from bottom to top.

"At least, you still look so pretty. You're so stunning. That's the reason why I fell in love with you, *Little one*," he said, dragging out the last two words. My phone started to buzz. I knew that was Sydney, most likely wondering that something terribly wrong had to be happening with me.

Still, I didn't know if he was going to show up here or not. He might not. After all, he didn't know me well, and I was pretty certain that he thought little of me. All he thought was that I was someone who didn't know anything about what I was doing, and I was also totally awkward with him, and I was certain that was something he still found funny.

I spat on Jason's face. It was the only thing I could do. I couldn't hurt him physically, and that would have been a wasted effort anyway.

Without thinking about anything that he should do, he whirled around, still holding me, and then he threw me onto the couch. At least, he had the decency of doing that. I thought that he was going to throw me against the wall. Had he done that, I would certainly have passed out.

"You have nothing to fear, Gloria. I'm here to protect you. As your Daddy, that's what I have to do. That's what I will always have to do. You are the most important person in the world to me and I want you to know that."

I had no idea what he had in mind, but I didn't like it anyway.

I opened my mouth in a heartbeat and I was going to scream. I was going to scream as loud as possible so that one of the neighbors could hear me.

But just when I was going to do that, I heard a car pulling over by the sidewalk. Then, the door opened and, less than five seconds after that, the door to my living room burst open, and I glanced at the person that was there.

This was it. It was him. He was my savior and he was going to keep me protected from this monster that was in my house.

His name was Sydney and he was like a superhero right now.

# CHAPTER 5

*Sydney*

"What the fuck are you doing here and who are you?" He asked, stepping toward me, but the way he walked showed me that he was drunk. He could barely keep his balance. He almost tripped and fell over when he was walking on the carpet.

I had no idea who he was, but he was so drunk that his cheeks were slightly blushing. Not to mention the terrible smell coming from his mouth, too. It made my stomach churn.

And he was holding a knife, which he was now pointing at me. He had it pointed at Gloria.

Right now, she was finally standing up. She put the towel around her body, and I couldn't help but think that it was a pity she did that. She was so stunning and, wow... I couldn't wrap my head around the chain of events that were going on here. A moment before this, I was driving here and now I was in Gloria's house and there was this man who looked a little younger than me.

He was threatening me with the knife, and if he thought that was going to be enough to stop me, he had something coming.

"I'm here to save Gloria from you, apparently. I'm going to give you a chance to wait here for the sheriff. I'm sure that he will want to lock you up."

"I'm not going to wait for Victor," he said, the way that he talked, so slow, dragging out the words, showed me once more that he was drunk a lot more than I had ever been in my life.

He could hit me with the knife, and he actually just tried to do that. He thrust it against my chest and he would have been able to hurt me with it if I didn't have my SEAL training. So, I dodged my body out of the way, and then I kicked him on the side of his body, taking the knife out of his hand. Just like that. My movements were fast like a lightning bolt.

"How the hell did you manage to do that?" He growled, palming his right hand with his left hand, showing me that I had hurt him. Good. I wanted to hurt him.

"I'm a SEAL. Or was. Anyway, it doesn't matter. You are going to wait here for the sheriff and then you are going to jail."

"A SEAL, huh? You think that I'm going to be impressed by something like that?" He said, trying to kick me, but I was able to deflect his attempts. It was quite easy to do that, and I suddenly found myself feeling this rush of adrenaline pumping in my body even though this moment was a far cry from everything that happened back when I was in the Middle East.

"I didn't say anything about that. I just want to make sure that Gloria is going to be safe."

"And who are you to her? Her new boyfriend or something like that?" He asked, trying to punch me, and this time I decided to end this before it was too late. It wasn't even a contest. One moment his fist was flying in the air and then, the next, he was knocked out on the floor, his eyes having rolled inside his head.

Gloria gasped and I turned so that I was looking at her. I approached her and grabbed her hand. This was my way to comfort her and I could tell that it was working. She looked up, finding my eyes, and there was this moment when I thought she was going to kiss me.

It was at this moment when everything around us seemed to be frozen.

But I knew that it was silly. The kind of girl I was looking for, even though it could be her, I knew that it wasn't her. After all, she couldn't be a Little, and that was more than obvious.

"What's going to happen now?" She asked and when I was

going to answer her question, I decided to do something else.

"Put on your clothes. I think that you need to look decent now. The sheriff is going to show up soon. I'm going to call him and explain everything that happened."

But just when I was going to turn around and do that, we heard hurried footsteps bolting out of the house. And I knew that I had made a mistake. A mistake that I couldn't forgive myself for, and that was putting it mildly.

It was him, who I was assuming to be her ex. He was running out of the house and was fast like a bullet train. He was so much faster than I thought someone like him could be.

"Oh, you are not going anywhere," I promised myself, but just when I was going to do that, I felt Gloria's hand grabbing mine. She held me in place. I turned around in a heartbeat, finding her.

"What are you doing, Gloria? I need to go. I need to go and drag his ass back here. I need to make sure that the police will lock him up. He can't be allowed out in society anymore. He's a danger to everyone."

"I know, but I also know who he is. He is my ex. His name is Jason and he is still thinking about me. He is obsessed with me. He thinks that we shouldn't have broken up. So, it's fine, even though it could be better. When Victor comes here, we are going to tell him everything and he will assemble a search party to find Jason. I'm sure that they will eventually find him, wherever he is right now."

I couldn't completely understand her reasons, but there was something about it that told me she actually wanted me here because she didn't want to be alone. If I left after Jason, she would be alone until the sheriff came, and... It was fine, I supposed.

It just didn't mean that I had to like it.

# CHAPTER 6

*Gloria*

So, the man who I thought wasn't going to show up, did. He was here with me in my house, and the sheriff was also here with us. He had his hands on his waist and was looking at Sydney with questioning eyes. He had to be questioning himself about what was happening here, as he should be. He was the sheriff, after all.

"So, you're telling me that you can't leave a cruiser parked in front of her house to protect her?" Sydney asked, sounding like he couldn't believe what Victor had told him, and neither could I.

After all, he was telling me that he didn't have enough deputies under his command to keep at least one of them patrolling the perimeter of my house.

"It's just as I said. I don't have enough men and certainly not enough cruisers to spare one of them so that she can be protected. I know it's not ideal, but there's no way around it. You are just going to have to accept it."

"That's bullshit and you know it!" Sydney shouted, sounding angry. He should be angry. After all, the sheriff himself was telling us that protecting me was not an option.

I could see it in his face, though. He wanted to keep one of the cruisers in front of the house, but he just couldn't do it, which meant that we were going to have to come up with a different solution. I couldn't imagine myself sleeping in my bedroom anymore without feeling worried, all the time, about

Jason coming back.

He was unhinged, the kind of man that we couldn't predict. We didn't know what he was going to do next. All we knew was that he wasn't going anywhere out of the city. If anything, he was going to stay here so that he could come after me again.

I wasn't saying that he would, but I still knew that the possibility would always be present until the day when he was locked up in a prison cell.

"It's not bullshit," the sheriff explained. "You said before that you don't have a job and that you were a SEAL. I think that you could be her protection. You could keep her protected, if you care so much about her."

My eyes widened in an instant. I didn't think that Victor was going to propose something like that.

Sydney living with me? I couldn't wrap my head around it. It was unbelievable.

I started to mumble and Sydney looked at me, his eyes questioning me. He was examining my facial expression. He wanted to know if I was okay with that.

To be honest about it, part of me was. Part of me was okay with it, but another part of me didn't want it. I didn't want it because I didn't think that it would be good for me.

After all, I would never be able to resist so many things that would sprout up the moment he started living with me.

"I can do that if she's okay with it," he said without showing surprise. Unlike me, he was not torn about it.

"I don't know if I-" I tried to say but I immediately stopped myself from continuing my words before it was too late.

"You sure? Because, I really don't mind," he insisted, and now I felt like I was throwing away what might be the opportunity of my life. Not to mention that he would most likely find out about my playroom and I wouldn't have as much freedom as I had now to be who I was when people couldn't see me.

I took a deep breath in, eventually replying, "I suppose there is no harm in doing that." And I felt like I was making the worst mistake of my life, but that it was a good one, too. I mean, that stunning, jaw-dropping SEAL was going to be living with me and I never thought I would find myself in this situation.

"Looks like everything here is settled, then," Victor said, turning around and picking up the call after his phone's ringtone started. "Yes, Jackie, is there anything you need me to pick up from the supermarket?"

Who was Jackie? I asked myself, realizing that it didn't matter. I didn't know her and certainly didn't feel like meeting anyone new right now.

Sydney walked over to me. "If you don't want to do this, it's fine. We can ask someone else to come over and stay with you until Jason is locked up."

I waved my hand, stepping away from him. At least now I was dressed, I thought, feeling relieved. Jason couldn't see me naked.

"No, it's fine, like I said. I don't really mind it," And even though I was keeping a serious, controlled expression about this, the truth was that, on the inside, my mind was going haywire.

After a moment of silence, when I didn't know what to say, he asked, "should I sleep on the couch? Wouldn't be the first time…"

I whirled around in the same instant, bulging out my eyes. "You don't have to," I said when I realized that there was no other option. It was either that or sleeping with me in my bed, or finding out about my crib, and the latter couldn't happen at all. I wasn't going to let it.

"Then, couch it is," he said, flopping onto the couch and pulling out his phone, most likely telling his family that tonight and in all the nights following this one, he was going to be sleeping right here under my roof.

My heart was still speeding up. I was beyond excited at this point.

# CHAPTER 7

*Sydney*

So, here I was, living in her house and it was the first night. Gloria was sleeping in her bed and I just realized that there was something about this that was nagging me slightly. I couldn't stop thinking about it. I was getting obsessed with it, and it was making me feel horrible about myself.

Even though I didn't have the right to know about what was in that room, I still wanted to know. I still wanted to know everything about Gloria because she made me feel something different about her.

But I supposed that that didn't matter at all right now. I said that because the hours were passing and Jason hadn't shown up yet. Well, I supposed that he wasn't going to show up so soon after that incident. Not to mention that he probably had to heal his wounds. I did give him a good beating that he would never forget, after all.

I was sleeping on her couch, or at least I was pretending I was. So many things happened tonight that I couldn't close my eyes without fearing that something terrible might happen. I did bring up to Gloria that she needed to close her window shut and that she couldn't open it no matter what happened.

She agreed with me, and I knew that she was going to keep her word.

It still didn't mean that I had to think that everything was going to be okay tonight, though.

One thing that I found curious about all this was that the other room – the one that she didn't want me to get into – wasn't her bedroom. She said that there was nothing of importance in there, items that she didn't need anymore.

If that was the case, then why was she keeping the door locked from me? I didn't know, but now that I was thinking more about it, I was even more curious about what might be in there. I wasn't stupid. This was far from the first time someone was trying to lie to me, and well… There was no point in ever bringing it up to Gloria. I didn't want to hurt her, no matter what happened.

And then, I started to hear something weird coming from her bedroom. I got off the couch in a heartbeat. If something was wrong with her and she needed my help, then I had to help her, just like I said I was going in all the other times that was brought up.

So, without thinking twice about it, I headed over to her bedroom. The noises that I was hearing were just her moaning and groaning. For a moment, I didn't think anything about it, but then I thought that perhaps she was using a dildo to get off right in the middle of the night.

It wouldn't be surprising if that was what was happening. After all, she needed to wind down a little after everything that happened.

So, I decided to step away from the door, but then I heard something else. Something that made my heart skip a beat. She was sobbing. *Gloria was crying.*

My heart was broken after hearing that. I couldn't see anyone, much less a woman, crying and sobbing without me doing something about it. So, I knocked on the door and it stopped.

That was a typical reaction. She'd thought that she had the privacy to cry and sob without anyone hearing anything. But the problem was that I was here in her house and the walls were like they were made of paper.

So, I knocked on the door again, hoping that she was going to let me in. I wasn't forcing her to do that. The only thing I was thinking about was that, right now, she needed my support.

Seconds later, when it was obvious that she wasn't going to answer and was actually going to keep pretending she didn't hear my knocking on the door, I decided to say, "Gloria, I know it's you. I know that you're crying and going through something horrible. I want you to understand that I'm here for you and everything else you need."

"I'm not crying. It's just that there is something in my eye and I can't seem to get rid of it."

That was the most bullshit excuse I'd heard in a very long time, but I wasn't going to say that, of course.

"Do you want to talk with me about what happened? What happened between you and your ex… I know that you can't forget about it easily. I'm here to offer you my support. You will probably feel better when I'm inside your room with you."

A minute later, she didn't answer and I didn't hear her footsteps coming to the door. I sighed, turning around, and I was going to leave when I started to hear her footsteps nearing the door. I was surprised, my eyes going wide. Some seconds later, Gloria opened the door and she was standing in the doorway, looking at me as though she wanted to tell me so much, but couldn't.

There was this moment of silence where we didn't say anything to each other. My heart sank in my chest. She looked so distressed, so beaten, and so weak that I just had to do something about this before it was too late.

And then, she broke down, the tears flowing free from her eyes, and I knew I had to do something. So, I wrapped my arms around her body, pulling Gloria close to me and settling my chin on top of her head. I was tall enough in comparison to Gloria to make that happen without having to go on my tiptoes.

And she was crying on my chest and I could feel the way that she was hugging me so tightly.

"It's okay. You can tell me everything. I'm here to keep you protected, even from your thoughts."

# CHAPTER 8



So, this was happening and I couldn't stop it anymore. My arms were wrapped around his body and I could feel the heat, his body, and the way that he was comforting me. I didn't have anyone else here with me. I could have my aunt, but she was actually traveling somewhere else and was so far away from me she couldn't come here, even though she knew about everything that happened and had promised that she was going to be here as soon as she could. So, I wasn't worried about not having company. What I was worried about was Jason showing up here again if we let our guards down.

But that wasn't going to happen as long as I had Sydney. He was holding me so tightly and his body was so incredibly warm. I didn't want to move away from him even though I should. After all, after feeling the comfort and warmth of his body, and also hearing the beating of his heart, I had already stopped crying and was feeling so much better.

So, I should be moving away, but I didn't want to. He was looking and acting so much like a Daddy I just wanted this to go on forever. I didn't even want to go to work tomorrow. I didn't have to, but I had said to my boss that the incident with Jason didn't affect me so much. But the truth was that it did and it showed. It showed in my tears, the way that I was crying, the way that my body was shaking, and the way that I felt so lonely. He was the only one giving me support, and as for that crush I had on him before?

It was so much more than that right now. It was beginning to turn into love.

I finally looked up when he moved his head away from the top of my head.

He brushed his hand on my cheek, saying, "I'm here for you. I'm here to keep you protected. If that asshole shows up here again, I'll beat the shit out of him so bad that he will think a million times before ever thinking about doing anything similar to another person. He'll regret ever being born."

I chuckled at his semi-joke, moving away from him even though, again, my body was begging me not to do that. I just didn't want to look so desperate and that I was so lonely.

I sat on my bed and he sat there with me. He put his arm around me, over my shoulders, and I just knew he was going to do that. The worry he felt for me was all over his face.

More and more, he looked like a true Daddy, and I just wanted all of this to turn into something else.

"I'm so sorry that you heard me crying. I didn't think that you were going to hear it. I think that, when I feel better, I'm going to soundproof the walls of my house."

"Hey, don't worry about it. It's okay to cry. It's okay to look for support when you need it. You are going through a lot and it shows. I just want to make sure that you really have everything you need and that you can tell me everything. I know I'm a stranger to you. Basically, the only thing you know about me is that I was a SEAL and that I did some operations in the Middle East, but you can ask me anything, and you can tell me anything. I'm going to keep my lips sealed about all your secrets."

I examined his eyes and I knew that he was telling me the truth. It was his friendliness, his kindness, the way that he was being sweet to me right now that was making me think we could really be so much more than who we were to each other right now. He was my bodyguard, in a way, and I was his protected one.

"I'm sorry, but I don't think that I should really tell you

anything about how I'm really feeling about this."

He lowered his voice when he said, "maybe I shouldn't be saying this, but I think that you are special. I think that you are the most amazing woman in the world, and ever since meeting you today in front of that café, I can't stop thinking about you. You know what? I'm going to be blunt about this. I have a crush on you. You make me feel something I thought I would never feel."

My eyes glistened with so many things going on in my mind. He just said that. He just said that he had a crush on me, and that was another step taken toward us becoming more than what we were right now.

Perhaps we could be lovers. I didn't know anything about that, but I did know that my heart was beating fast right now and I was a little vulnerable – more so than normal, and I couldn't help but wonder what it would be like to kiss him for the first time. To feel his sweet, intense lips on mine, his tongue going inside, looking for the interior of our mouths, our saliva getting mixed, his lips rubbing and pressing on mine, and… and I knew I was just daydreaming.

It wasn't like any of that was going to happen.

I was just thinking that impossible things were going to happen when it was likely that they could never.

So, I didn't do anything, but then I felt his lips nearing mine, and it wasn't too long until we were kissing. It was one of the best kisses of my life, especially because I had only kissed my ex before, and he wasn't such a good kisser. Actually, in comparison to Sydney, he was terrible.

I was letting this happen and I wasn't fighting it. I actually wanted this to continue.

# CHAPTER 9

*Gloria*

He pulled his head back, looking at me with questioning eyes. "Do you feel okay right now, Gloria? Do you want me to go on?" Sydney asked and I appreciated that he did that. The kiss was mesmerizing and breathtaking. Now that he kissed me, I couldn't even think about Jason and all the things that he brought with him.

I was only thinking about me and Sydney.

"I don't think we should. I don't want something to happen that shouldn't. There's something about me that nobody should ever know."

"What kind of thing?" He asked, brushing a lock of my hair behind my ear, doing that slowly and so sexily. He knew what he was doing. He knew how to let his fingers just slide slowly over the skin of my head, letting me feel the softness of his skin.

I shook my head. "Never mind. Just kiss me already. Kiss me as many times as you want to," I told him and he did exactly what I asked of him. Our lips connected again, his mouth crashing against mine, and it was so much better than anything I had before.

Our kiss was slow but extremely passionate at the start. I could feel his lips every so often pressing, rubbing, pushing against mine, and I didn't want to go anywhere. I closed my eyes and allowed myself to be immersed in this moment.

My body was beginning to get hot.

It was obvious that Sydney noticed my reaction, for he soon was putting his fingers under my shirt, and then he lifted it up and over my head. I didn't have much say in that. He wanted to see me naked, and he was getting exactly that.

He chucked the shirt over his head, allowing his eyes to feast on my naked body. He started to mumble something and when he realized that I couldn't understand what he said, he made it clearer, "you are amazing. I mean, I've always known that you are, but now that I can see the real thing in person, well… I feel like I'm in heaven."

I didn't know about *him* being in heaven, but I felt like I was. His fingers moving over my body, pressing on all the right spots, making me crazy, making me tilt my head back and close my eyes again. The way that his hands were feeling me and touching me was something I would never forget.

Sweat was beginning to pool on my forehead.

He must've noticed how much I was giving myself to him, for in a moment he put his hands around my back and unhooked my bra. It happened before I could say anything about it. One moment the bra was covering my breasts and then the next it was gone. After reopening my eyes one more time, I found myself with my bust completely exposed, and I still just wanted this to keep going on.

"As I said, you are the most beautiful woman I've ever seen," he said one more time, and every time that he complimented me on my looks, I felt goosebumps all over my body. I felt my skin getting hotter.

"Hmmm," was all I could mutter. I knew that he was smiling. That cocky smile that only he could pull off.

Sydney planted his hands on my boobs, moving them, pressing them into the skin, massaging them, and making me moan and groan as I forgot about every terrible thing that happened since this all started between us. I couldn't even remember Jason and the fact that he was still on the loose.

Sydney pulled his hands back. For a moment, I didn't

understand why he did that, but then it became obvious to me. He had something else in mind. He snuck his fingers under my shorts and then he lowered them, exposing my legs and my waist to the delight of his eyes. They glistened under the moonlight coming through the window.

"Good Lord, you are even more beautiful and stunning," he murmured and then he looked into my eyes as if he was asking himself if I was okay with the thing that he wanted to do now. And how could I not be? I asked myself when I nodded and he had the permission he was looking for.

Without saying anything else, he widened his smile, and then he removed my panties. I knew he was going to do that. I pressed my legs together as if I was afraid he was going to hurt me, but it was obvious that he was not going to do anything of the sort.

Sydney was actually being extremely careful with me.

He ran his fingers on my pussy, scratching my clit slowly. "You like it when I do this to you, don't you?" He asked and I nodded. Of course I liked every moment of this. I liked the fact that he was bringing me so close to my orgasm even though not much was happening here yet.

After looking down, I could see it. I could see the growing bulge under his pants. He was hard. Much more so than probably ever before in his life, and after giving it another glance, it became obvious to me that he was so big I doubted that he could even fit inside of me.

But I didn't say anything about that. What I did was think a little more about how well he was playing with my pussy folds and grazing his finger on my clit. The way that he did all those things shot shockwaves of pleasure in my body, and I felt like I was almost on the verge of passing out.

Perhaps he was going to do that, or perhaps he had another plan in mind.

Either way, I didn't know and the only thing I actually knew about this was how much I wanted to see Sydney naked.

After all, after seeing him for the first time in front of the café, the only thing I was wondering about now was how stunning he was without his clothes on.

And now that we were sharing this moment together, that little wish of mine just might turn real...

# CHAPTER 10

*Gloria*

So, here I was and he was all over me. His fingers pressing, exploring, looking, doing everything possible to bring me as much pleasure as he could. It was almost impossible not to give in to the temptation – the temptation that we were going to finish this the only way that we could, with him orgasming inside of me.

"You're so beautiful and you deserve every moment of this," he murmured, bending his body and putting his head right in front of my pussy. I felt my legs quivering. I knew what Sydney wanted to do, and I was giving him the opportunity to make his wish real.

"I'm going to make you so happy right now, Gloria," he murmured, licking, rubbing, and dancing with his tongue all over my pussy lips. His saliva mixed with the liquid that was already coming out, and I felt like I was going to pass out. My hips felt so weak like they were made of glass, and his fingers were still sliding all over my legs, looking for my asscheeks and then, without giving me a warning, he cupped them, bringing me a little closer to him.

Close enough so that he could do something that I thought he wasn't.

Sydney buried his head between my legs and in my pussy. I felt his tongue slashing and dancing all over my pussy folds, and then he did something that not even I, with a mind as dirty as mine, thought he was going to.

He slid his tongue into my cunt. Just like that, without as much as giving me a warning.

He kept it there for a long time, eventually taking it out when he felt that it was enough. And to think that this was only the first night with him and that there were so many more still to come… I felt like I was in heaven.

In a moment, Sydney finally did the thing that I'd been waiting for all this time. He peeled off his clothes, showing me his mesmerizing, mouthwatering body, and I didn't know what to do other than to check it out from bottom to top, trying to find something wrong with it, but soon realizing that I couldn't. He was perfect like that, and I couldn't believe that he was doing all of this.

Even though this might be crossing my mind only thanks to the rush of the moment, I couldn't help but wonder if he was more open-minded and I could tell him my secret. That I was a Little.

I didn't have much time to do that, though.

In a moment, he got a condom from the pocket of his pants. I didn't even know that he had it with him there, as if he was suspecting that he was going to fuck me tonight. He put it on his cock, grabbed my thighs, and then penetrated me slowly, making sure that his eyes were on me all the time, ascertaining himself that I wasn't feeling too much pain.

And in truth, I wasn't.

"Oh, Daddy. You love me so much," I let that out, the first time in a very long time that I let my guard down, and I would be regretting it if it wasn't for the fact that I couldn't even think like I normally would be if circumstances were different.

"I knew you were going to say that," he said, pounding in and out of me, doing that slowly in the beginning, and then he picked up the pace when he was more used to my size.

I had no idea what he meant by that, but it was obvious that it didn't change the way that he thought about this. Sydney continued to do what he was doing. He continued to pound in and out of me, and I continued to squeal, moan, groan, and do a lot of other things I never thought I would be doing with another man.

Seconds later, Sydney erupted. His cock started to squirm and shake violently in my pussy, and I clenched my walls tight around him to make sure that he wasn't going to go anywhere. It was a pity that he wasn't shooting that load directly on my walls, but I wasn't going to say anything about it. I could feel his cock pressing against and rubbing on my g-spot, and it was so entrancing and everything else that I felt my climax coming, and, when it did, it washed over my entire body like a massive wave.

My chest was panting. I reopened my eyes one more time so that I could see what was happening around me. Sydney was still on top of me and even after he finished inside of me, he remained exactly where he was. His dick stretched my pussy so wide I doubt it would ever return to normal, not that it mattered, anyway.

He lied down by my side, his arm around me. Our lips connected one more time for another kiss, and then he said, "I never thought I would be saying this. I had always thought that there was no such thing as love and I wasn't really looking forward to it, and I know it's crazy since we've been together for so little time, but I think that I'm really in love with you, and I hope that I'm not the only one who feels that way about us. I want you to understand that."

I kissed him one more time. This time, it was just a peck.

"I do love you. I love you so much and, as I said, I know it's crazy to think about you this way after spending so little time together. I think that there is something about me you should know and I know I'm taking a huge risk, but I also feel that we can't go on without being completely honest to each other."

He nodded once and slowly, giving me the comfort and the confirmation I was looking for. So, in the end, I didn't have much of a reason to worry that Sydney was going to dump me the moment when I revealed my true self to him.

I slid out of the bed, putting on a robe while still feeling like he was still inside of me. "Come. There's something that I need to show you. I know that you've been thinking about it all this time, and I think that I trust you enough to show it to you."

Sydney didn't say anything about this, but there was no

denying that he was excited about the prospect of finally stepping inside my hidden room.

"Going right there with you now," he said, coming in tow. I got the key, opened the door, and stepped inside the room with him. I was where I was, wondering what was going on in his mind right now. He had to be thinking that something was deeply wrong with me.

This room, with this decoration, all the 'silly' and childish toys, the teddy bear, the collection of pacifiers, and even the diapers. I hoped that he was beginning to understand why, before, I said what I said, that he was my Daddy not because of any daddy issues – other than the ones I had with Jason – but because I saw him as the Daddy for the Little I was.

"Oh, Gloria. I didn't think that you are a Little. This whole time, I've been wondering if I would ever find the right person, the one that understood me, the one that was a Little so that I could be more than her boyfriend, and here you are showing me that I can make all of that real. You are amazing, and I don't feel like I'm repeating myself by saying that."

I blinked twice, not believing the words coming out of his mouth. Sydney was a Daddy? He turned around, meeting me, and then I threw myself into his arms, letting them envelop me. And I kissed him again and again, and as many times as possible until we were both gasping for air and our bodies were all sweaty again.

"And I didn't think you were a Daddy," I said, tears coming out of my eyes and I couldn't stop them. They rolled down my cheeks, and I found myself increasingly pushing myself into his body, letting our hug turn into something I would never forget.

"I am. This whole time, I've been wondering if you are a Little, and I'm beyond happy that you are."

Sydney kissed me again, and then I went over to my crib. He was right behind me and, this time, he had his arm around my waist. It was like he was telling me that no matter what happened, he was going to keep me safe.

But just when we were going to continue our little adventure in my playroom, we heard a noise that made us jump where we were. It came from the living room, and it couldn't be more obvious what it meant.

It had to be Jason. He had to have come here for me again, even though it was a mistake, even though he was hurt, and even though he shouldn't be here at all.

It was for this reason that the sheriff should have kept a patrol cruiser in front of the house.

But now, it was too late for that, and I was certain that even Sydney understood that. He put his hand on my chest, saying, "I know that it's Jason that has just come here, and this time I'm not going to make the same mistake."

Alarmed by his words, the first thought that came into my mind was that he was going to kill Jason. Thinking that, I grabbed his hand before he did what would be the biggest mistake of his life.

"Please, don't kill him. I'm going to call Victor. He is going to come here quickly and you will put Jason behind bars. I'm certain of it."

"Call him. Tell me what's going on. In the meantime, I'm going to deal with that intruder," he said, keeping the door shut behind him, but he didn't lock it with the key.

I dialed the numbers to call Victor and he picked up the call, and I told him everything. I told him about everything going on here and he said that he was going to come right now. It was only going to take him a handful of minutes, and I was already waiting for him.

And I couldn't stay in my playroom for too long. The fight between Jason and Sydney had already started and, if he needed my help, I had to go there before it was too late.

But just when I arrived in the living room, Jason was already on the floor, his legs and arms spread out, his eyes having rolled inside his head, and this time Sydney was on top of him, his knee on his chest.

He looked up, smirking. "I've got this. This time, I'm not going to take my eyes off him."

And I knew that he wasn't going to make the same mistake

twice.

Just like I had thought, it was only minutes later when the sheriff and some deputies arrived in their cruisers, and... at long last Jason was going to be locked up behind bars.

I had always thought that I would never fall in love again after breaking up with my ex, but Sydney was showing me something different. He was showing me that there was indeed love and that I could give it another chance.

He kissed me again while the police cruiser took Jason to prison. This time, he was going to be locked up for a long time and I didn't have to worry about him anymore.

# SYDNEY'S EPILOGUE

John was with me. He was my childhood friend, and he was also a Daddy. He was a Daddy that couldn't find his little. We were having a barbecue at Gloria's place, and I was the one flipping the burgers, conditioning the meat, and preparing some other things. The smell in the air was delicious, making my stomach growl in hunger.

"So, you're telling me that you met up with Gloria by luck? You helped her fix her car?" He asked, lifting his hand, the one that was holding the beer can, and taking a sip from it.

"That's right. That's what happened."

Just over his shoulder, there she was. She was outside, having a picnic with her aunt and a friend that she made recently. Her friend's name was Jackie and she was the sheriff's Little and girlfriend.

Now that I was thinking about it, it was kind of crazy, wasn't it? I had once thought, in a town as small as this one, that things like Littles didn't exist, but now it was all proving me otherwise. It was all showing me that there were Littles around and I couldn't help but wonder if that meant that even John was going to find his promised one.

"Wow," he said, looking down. Even though he would never admit it to me, he was jealous. He was jealous that I found someone I was happy with and someone that I was going to live the rest of my life with. "You were so lucky. I don't think that I can ever find someone that's like her. Gloria really is someone to treasure for the rest of your life."

"She really is," I said, finishing the preparations where the barbecue was being made and then waving over my head before yelling, "barbecue is ready, everyone! You can eat now."

And after saying that, they all shot up from the picnic mat on the grass and came right over in a heartbeat.

"Daddy, but this is so awesome. I want to eat everything. It really all looks so delicious," she said, but I had to be a killjoy and wiggle my finger in front of her face, showing that Gloria couldn't eat the barbecue. This was food for the adults.

"I think that you're going to eat something else. Something more appropriate for a Little like you," I warned and she pouted, showing her discontent with my decision, but it wasn't like it was going to change anything.

I was just so happy that we were together.

Now, it was time to give her favorite barbecue food to her even though she would never admit that to me.

She always tried to make me believe that she could and wanted to eat the food that was for the adults.

# GLORIA'S EPILOGUE

"Come on, roll over," he commanded and I did exactly what he wanted. I rolled over onto the diaper that was on the bed. It was a fresh, new diaper, and it was going to replace the old one. I had dirtied the old one with my pee, and it was smelly and I hated it.

But now, now that my butt was touching the new diaper, I already felt invigorated. I felt that I could face anything and everything now that I was going to have my diaper changed.

Daddy was the one that was going to do it. He already had everything he was going to need. Talcum, cream to make my skin less sensitive to the slight rash of the diaper, and a couple of other things. He was already applying them, even.

I felt his fingers moving over my pussy, and even though I shouldn't be feeling this way, they were turning me on. I didn't want to have an orgasm right during my diaper change, but if things remained this way, there wouldn't be much I would be able to do about it.

"You are really excited about this, aren't you?" He asked, smirking. Of course that he was going to bring out that cocky smirk of his. He was always so overconfident that sometimes he could be slightly irritating. Nevertheless, at the moment, he was anything but.

He was so sexy, I thought, his fingers playing with my pussy folds as if he owned them. The way that he was moving his fingers, sometimes flicking his index finger on my clit - it was all making me reach that point of no return. As I said, I didn't want to have an orgasm right now, but it just might happen, especially given the way that he was tormenting me with his digitals.

He was just so experienced when it came to this.

"Daddy!" I said loudly, but he still continued, and minutes later, it finally happened. My body started to convulse and I couldn't stop it anymore. My juices were coming out and dirtying the diaper, and now I couldn't walk around the house with a dirty diaper, much less one that smelled of my orgasm.

Even though... Even though I was certain that Daddy found that a huge turn-on for him. That was obvious in the way that he was leering at me.

"Oh, Little One. Look at the mess you made," he said, his tone showing discontentment and that he was about to punish me – I hoped that it was a spanking session – for being naughty. But really, this was all his fault.

"I'm sorry, Daddy. I promise that it won't happen again," I still said.

"You really promise with everything you have?"

I nodded.

I promised.

And it was so much more than that. I promised him that nothing would ever separate him and that, in the coming months, we were going to work on showing everyone our love.

Who we truly were.

*The End*

Don't forget to check the next page for a sneak peek to 'Sheriff's Feisty Little' and other stories by me.

# TEASER: SHERIFF'S FEISTY LITTLE

*Duty Calls - 1*

Honestly, I had no idea what I was doing in this bar. I thought that it was going to make me feel better, but it was actually doing the opposite. I felt worse just being in this place.

I felt like everyone was watching me, even though I was doing nothing more than just taking sips from the cheap beer can I was holding in my hand.

And, it was no surprise that everyone was going to be looking at me because I was the only girl in this place.

I was the only girl in the bar and I didn't think that was going to change in the foreseeable future. Looking around me, I could see that this was the kind of dive bar that most girls my age never went to.

It was a little unsettling, but I was beginning to get used to the feeling. I felt angry, though, thinking about the guys that stared at me. They all thought that they could have a chance with me, didn't they?

Of course they did.

Just taking another glance at everyone that was in the place, I knew that they thought they were way more than who they were.

They were actually nothing more than old, forgotten men that nobody wanted anymore, and that fact alone made me feel a little disgusted that I was still in this place and not somewhere else, where I could feel a little better.

I took another sip from the beer can I was holding in my hand. Perhaps I should tell the bartender that his beer's taste was terrible, but I wasn't that heartless, even though sometimes I felt like being that way.

Although I couldn't really help it sometimes, there was no denying that having a rage outburst was never a good thing, and I just didn't want to ruin the reputation I had already built for myself in this city.

Could I even call it a 'city,' though? I asked myself, realizing that the question was rather pointless at the moment.

The fact was that I was living here, didn't have any friends, and also didn't have a family. I also wasn't thinking about building a family here anytime soon because I was a Little and I knew that there were no Daddies around.

I knew that with so much certainty that it hurt me just thinking about it. I had already checked the Daddies Find Littles app, and it was how I knew that there were no Daddies around.

That was why I wasn't holding my breath when I noticed that one of those greasy men started to approach me. He had such a devilish smile on his face that I already knew what he was going to say before he did, and that stench coming out of his mouth as well... It made my stomach churn just thinking about it.

"Hello, pretty girl, what's a cute girl like you doing here?" He asked, checking me up and down as though I was some kind of trophy he could claim for himself. I didn't even have to ask him if that was exactly what he was thinking. I could read it in his expression, and it made me just want to slap his face until he begged for forgiveness.

But I knew that wasn't going to happen. He was so much bigger than me, and even though he had a dad body – cheap beer, big belly - I knew I would never stand a chance against him in a fair fight.

Not to mention that he was also surrounded by who I was

assuming to be his friends, and I didn't want anything to do with them as well. All in all, I just wanted to be leaving this place as soon as possible, but after he put his hand on the bar in front of me, I knew that wasn't possible anymore.

I lost my chance, I thought, feeling my rage bubbling in my veins.

He really thought that he was a hotshot, didn't he? I asked myself, turning my head around so that I could look perfectly at his eyes. He seemed so overconfident and his eyes showed me that he was piss drunk. His cheeks also told me the same thing, and that stench coming out of his mouth… It was like the more time passed, the stronger it got, and I hated that so much.

I was always angry and willing to stand up for myself, so what the hell was stopping me now from jumping off the stool where I was sitting and shouting that I didn't want anything to do with him? And much less that I wanted to talk to him?

I had no idea, but I supposed that it could be my sense of self-preservation that was doing that to me.

And if that were the case, then I was even angrier right now, though that would be more at me than the drunkard standing in front of me.

"I don't have anything to say to you," I grumbled, taking another sip from the beer can. I narrowed my eyebrows, glaring at the can as though I was going to throw it to the wall behind the bar. But I would never do that, especially because the bartender that had taken my order looked like a good guy, even though he didn't have much authority here in his bar, which was something that could defuse this situation in a heartbeat.

While I didn't know this for sure, I supposed that he was the owner's son.

"Are you sure about that?" The oily, nasty man asked, putting his hand on my shoulder, and it was at that moment that I stood up in a blink from the stool where I was sitting. "Because I know that look you gave me when you were checking me out before. You want me, don't you? You want my big cock in your wet pussy, don't you?"

I checked his crotch as he put his hand against it and pressed it up, sending shivers of absolute disgust in my body. Did he really think that what he just did was hot?

What a stupid question. I was sure he did, but it actually had the opposite effect on me, and I just couldn't stand what he'd just done.

He'd touched me. He had put his hand on my shoulder, felt my skin, and just thinking about that made my skin crawl.

He had crossed a boundary that I just couldn't… I just couldn't put up with what he did, and he was going to pay for it. That was why I just shoved down on the bar the cheap beer can and fisted my hand.

It wasn't just going to be a slap – it was actually going to be way more than that. I was going to punch him. I was going to punch him until his teeth were flying out of his mouth, and that was going to be the end of this.

He was even surprised by my reaction. He widened his eyes, but it was already too late.

And then… I realized that I had made a big mistake.

# SIMILAR BOOKS

# ABOUT THE AUTHOR

Amanda King writes sweet ABDL, age play romances. Packaged with steamy scenes, her books are fast-paced and, more often than not, they deeply explore the world of age gap relationships.

When she isn't writing, she's reading for inspiration. Some of her most popular stories are "Pampering Little Miguel" and "Endless Crayons."

9 7 9 8 8 4 6 1 5 9 7 9 2